Oh no, Woolly Bear!

A Lift-the-Flap Book

By Patricia McFadden   Illustrated by Michèle Coxon

STAR BRIGHT BOOKS

NEW YORK

Published in the United States of America by Star Bright Books, Inc., New York.
The name Star Bright Books and the Star Bright Books logo are registered
trademarks of Star Bright Books, Inc. Please visit www.starbrightbooks.com.

ISBN-13: 978-1-59572-149-5

LCCN: 2008926517

Printed in China (WKT) 9 8 7 6 5 4 3 2 1

The autumn wind blew.
The autumn leaves flew.
"B-r-r-r," said Woolly Bear Caterpillar.
"I'd better find a place to stay for
the winter."

Woolly Bear bristled and bustled along to the flower garden. He saw Bee getting nectar from an autumn aster.

"Hello, Bee," said Woolly Bear. "Where do you spend the winter?"

"I stay alive inside my hive," said Bee.

"May I stay with you?"
asked Woolly Bear.

Woolly Bear bristled and bustled along to the vegetable garden. He saw Ladybug sitting on a stalk of broccoli.

"Hello, Ladybug," said Woolly Bear. "Where do you spend the winter?"

"In piles of dozens, I doze with my cousins," said Ladybug.

"May I stay with you?"
asked Woolly Bear.

Woolly Bear bristled
and bustled to the woods.
He saw Spider hanging
from a staghorn
sumac.

"Hello, Spider," said Woolly Bear.
"Where do you spend the winter?"

"I curl up my legs and sleep by
my eggs," said Spider.

Woolly Bear bristled and bustled along to the meadow. He saw Ant carrying a brown burdock seed.

"Hello, Ant," said Woolly Bear. "Where do you spend the winter?"

"Inside my hill away from the chill," said Ant.

"May I stay with you?"
asked Woolly Bear.

Woolly Bear bristled and bustled along to the creek. He saw Dragonfly Nymph darting through ripples.

"Hello, Dragonfly Nymph," said Woolly Bear. "Where do you spend the winter?"

"Under the ice. It's cold there, but nice," said Dragonfly Nymph.

"B-r-r-r!" said
Woolly Bear.
"I don't want to
stay with you."

Woolly Bear was too tired to bristle, too cold to bustle. He saw Whirligig Beetle crawl out of the water.

"Hello, Whirligig Beetle," said Woolly Bear. "Where do you spend the winter?"

"I burrow down deep for a long, cozy sleep," said Whirligig Beetle.

"May I PLEASE stay with you?" asked Woolly Bear.

"Oh, yes, Woolly Bear," said Whirligig Beetle. "You're welcome to stay."

"Thank you," said Woolly Bear.

Whirligig scrinched. Woolly Bear scrunched.

"Good night," said Whirligig Beetle.

"Good night," said Woolly Bear.

Woolly Bear Caterpillar closed his eyes, went to sleep, and dreamed . . .